PUZZLE HOLIDAY

Susannah Leigh

Illustrated by Brenda Haw

Contents

Editor: Michelle Bates
Series Editor: Gaby Waters

KT-162-059

About this book

This book is about Katy and Tim and their trip to the Puzzle Holiday Park. Katy and Tim love puzzles. There is one for them to solve on every double page. Can you help them? If you get stuck you can look at the answers on pages 31 and 32.

Katy

Tim

Katy's and Tim's adventure began with an exciting package that landed on their doorstep. Inside the package was a letter from their friend Molly.

Molly

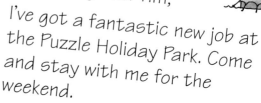

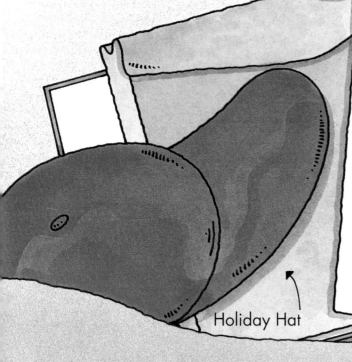

Holiday Hat

Dear Katy and Tim,

I've got a fantastic new job at the Puzzle Holiday Park. Come and stay with me for the weekend.

Catch the red and yellow Holiday Express bus from the town square at ten o'clock on Saturday morning.
See you soon!

Love
Molly

P.S. Special Holiday Hats are enclosed. Please wear them at all times.

Stinky skunks

There is at least one stinky skunk hiding on every double page from pages 6-7. Look out for them, but hold your nose!

2

Supreme Spotters' Challenge

There are all kinds of weird and wonderful things to see in and around the Puzzle Holiday Park. You will find them all listed below. There is something to spot on every double page. Collect the points as you go and add up your score at the end of your adventure to find out how you did.

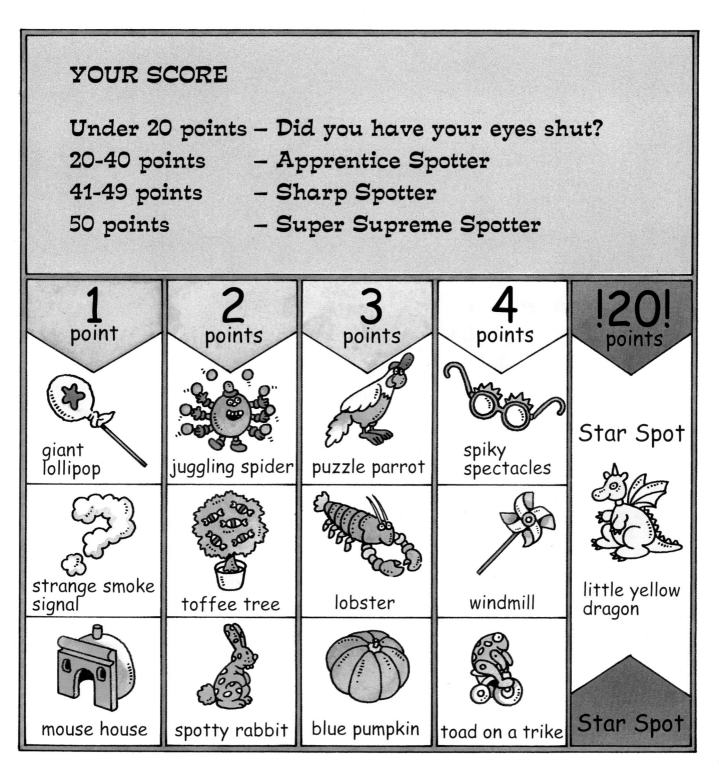

YOUR SCORE

Under 20 points – Did you have your eyes shut?
20-40 points – Apprentice Spotter
41-49 points – Sharp Spotter
50 points   – Super Supreme Spotter

1 point
giant lollipop
strange smoke signal
mouse house

2 points
juggling spider
toffee tree
spotty rabbit

3 points
puzzle parrot
lobster
blue pumpkin

4 points
spiky spectacles
windmill
toad on a trike

!20! points
Star Spot
little yellow dragon
Star Spot

Puzzle Holiday!

On Saturday morning at ten o'clock, Katy and Tim stood in the town square. They were very excited to be going to the Puzzle Holiday Park.

Katy and Tim wore their special Holiday Hats and looked around eagerly for the red and yellow Holiday Express bus.

"I can see an elephant in a truck and a monkey driving a car," said Tim.

"And there's a camper van with lots of luggage on the top," said Katy. "But where's our bus?"

Can you help Katy and Tim find the Holiday Express bus?

5

On the way

Katy and Tim climbed on board the Holiday Express bus.

"We'll pick up the other passengers on the way," the driver called.

And soon they were leaving the town far behind and driving through the countryside.

"Are all these people coming to the Holiday Park?" Katy and Tim cried as they stopped at a crossroads.

"Only the ones wearing special Holiday Hats like yours," grinned the driver.

Can you see who is going to the Holiday Park?

Listen carefully

At last they arrived at the Holiday Park. Molly came to meet them.

"Welcome everybody!" she called. "Now listen very carefully. I'm going to divide you up into four different groups. Each group will take part in all kinds of exciting activities. Read these instructions, then meet me at the campsite."

MAP OF PUZZLE HOLIDAY PARK
(mountain bike trail shown in orange)

FUNFAIR

GO-KARTING

CAMPSITE

ENTRANCE

BOATING LAKE

ANIMAL WORLD

WOODS

ARCHERY

BUMPY GROUND

FUN-SPLASH POOL

MUDDY RIVER

PRICKLY BUSHES

ARTS AND CRAFTS

SEASIDE FUN

ROLLER BLADING

CIRCUS SKILLS

Then Molly gave them all timetables and a map of the Park. Katy and Tim looked for their names and saw what activities their group would be doing that day.

What group are Katy and Tim in?
What activities will they be doing and what route will they have to take?

TODAY'S GROUPS

SCRAMBLERS: POPPY, ARCHIE, CARLA, BILLY
EXPLORERS: JAMES, CATH, MAX, SAM
PUZZLERS: KATY, TIM, GREG, SOPHIE
SPOTTERS: HARRY, BETH, ALEX, ROSIE

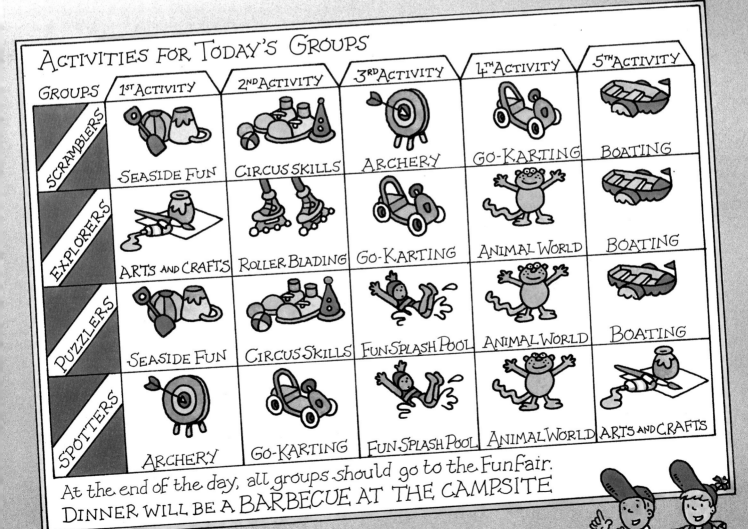

ACTIVITIES FOR TODAY'S GROUPS

GROUPS	1ST ACTIVITY	2ND ACTIVITY	3RD ACTIVITY	4TH ACTIVITY	5TH ACTIVITY
SCRAMBLERS	SEASIDE FUN	CIRCUS SKILLS	ARCHERY	GO-KARTING	BOATING
EXPLORERS	ARTS AND CRAFTS	ROLLER BLADING	GO-KARTING	ANIMAL WORLD	BOATING
PUZZLERS	SEASIDE FUN	CIRCUS SKILLS	FUN SPLASH POOL	ANIMAL WORLD	BOATING
SPOTTERS	ARCHERY	GO-KARTING	FUN SPLASH POOL	ANIMAL WORLD	ARTS AND CRAFTS

At the end of the day, all groups should go to the Funfair.
DINNER WILL BE A BARBECUE AT THE CAMPSITE

Tent trouble

Before the activities began, all the children went to the campsite. They saw tents and tepees, cabins and huts.

"Look at the pictures on the flags," Molly called. "Find the one that matches what you like doing best, and that's where you'll be sleeping tonight."

She turned away with a twinkle in her eye as everyone began to talk at once.

At last it was all figured out.

Listen to what everyone has to say. Can you see where they are all going to sleep?

11

Mountain bikes

When everyone had unpacked their bags, it was time for the fun to begin. Katy and Tim joined up with the other members of their group, Greg and Sophie. They looked at their timetable. Their first activity was at the seaside.

"You'll get there faster if you take the mountain bikes. Have fun," Molly said.

The Puzzlers grabbed their bikes.

They cycled over bumpy ground...

... across muddy rivers

...and through prickly bushes.

But then they stopped at a maze of paths. Which way should they go now? Other people were lost as well.

"Each path is scattered with clues!" Tim cried, looking at the ground. "It's easy to see where each one leads."

Can you find the paths everyone wants?

Seaside fun

The seaside was very busy. There were people everywhere! Katy and Tim and Sophie and Greg bounded onto the sand. They waved to the Scramblers.

"Come and build a sandcastle," called Beth, who was in charge of the beach. "It's a competition, but it isn't easy," she explained. "Each team's sandcastle has to include five blue pebbles, a feather, three red shells, some yellow seaweed and a flag. You've got half an hour to find everything on the beach. Go!"

Can you help find all the objects for both teams?

SANDCASTLE COMPETITION HERE

Half an hour later...

The sandcastles were finished. They were magnificent. But were they made with all the things that Beth had asked for?

Hillside scramble

The Puzzlers grinned, but the Scramblers groaned. They had left out one blue pebble.

"We'll beat you to the circus tent then," they cried as they raced off.

The Puzzlers raced after them, but the Scramblers had disappeared.

"There's the circus tent!" Greg pointed. "But we'll have to be careful how we get there. I can see some fallen rocks and log piles."

"And I've met some fearsome dragons before, but those wild animals look even scarier," Sophie shivered.

Can you find a safe way up the paths to the circus tent?

Circus fun

Quickly the children climbed safely up the hill. When they reached the top, they peered inside the circus tent.

"Come in Puzzlers," cried a brightly dressed figure. "I'm Jester Jim and I'll be teaching you how to juggle today. You can have a ride on the unicycles too, or even try your hand at plate spinning."

Before...

Then one of the clowns fired a cannon. BOOM! There was a puff of smoke and when it had cleared, things looked very different.

"Oh dear," wailed Jester Jim. "Everything's in a terrible muddle now. What's more, that loud noise made me drop all my juggling balls."

Can you spot all of the differences?

After...

Water fun

When everything was straightened out, the children headed for their next treat – the Fun Splash Pool! They gasped at the sight of the water chutes. Quickly, they changed into their bathing suits.

"Watch me splash into the bubble pit!" Greg said.

"I hope I land in the Ball Pond!" Katy called.

"I want to end up in the Wavy Water," Tim cried.

"It's Castaway Cove for me," Sophie cheered.

Which slides must each of them take if they want to end up in these places?

CASTAWAY COVE

BUBBLE PIT

Yahoo!

Animal world

Shaking their wet hair, the Puzzlers packed up their swimming things and left the Fun Splash Pool.

"I could have stayed there all day," said Katy. "But we've got to get to Animal World."

But when they got there, they found the farmer, Tilly, shaking her head. All the animals were mooing and neighing and baaing and oinking and clucking and quacking and squawking.

"It's feeding time," Tilly called above the din. "Now where did I put the parrots' seed cakes and the monkeys' bananas? I can't find the bread for the ducks or the chickens' sack of corn. What about the basket of hay for the goats, and a milk bottle for each lamb?"

"Don't worry, we'll find the food," Katy called.

Can you help them?

Boating lake

The children left the animals gobbling up their food and headed for the Boating Lake. Boats of all shapes and sizes were out on the water.

"I knew we'd be late," said Katy, stopping to tie her shoelace. "Even the Explorers are here already."

"It's all right," said Sophie. "Some of the boats are being called in. Listen."

Can you spot the boats which are being called in?

Time's up for the red boat number 12,
the yellow boat number 28,
the green boat number 6 and
the blue and white boat number 37.

25

Fun at the fair

An hour later, the Puzzlers' boat was called in.

"I'm starving. When's dinner?" Tim wailed, looking at his timetable.

"Not yet," Katy smiled. "We haven't been to the funfair."

Quickly, they ran there. Everyone wanted to go on different rides...

the bumper cars...

... the moon walk

... the spook train

... the merry-go-round

... the coconut shy.

"Look," Greg cried from the top of the wheel. "I can see our dinner cooking. It's time for the barbecue. Is everyone here?"

Are all the groups at the funfair?

Holiday feast

The children raced from the fairground to the barbecue. All kinds of delicious food was piled high. Tim's tummy rumbled.

"Hello everyone," Molly cried. "I hope you've had an exciting day. But before you start munching this lovely food, I have one more puzzle."

"Oh no," groaned Tim. "I'm starving!"

Molly smiled. "We've lost the toffee apples for dessert," she explained. "Can you find them all? There's one for all of you."

"Yum, yum," Tim cried. "That's one puzzle I don't mind solving!"

Can you find the toffee apples?

Starry night

That night, Katy and Tim lay snug in their tent and gazed up at the moon.

"What a wonderful time we've had," Katy sighed. "I don't think I've ever solved so many puzzles in one day."

"How did you do in the Supreme Spotters' Challenge?" Tim asked.

"I spotted everything," Katy said.

"So did I," said Tim. "That's 50 points."

"We're Super Supreme Spotters," Katy cried.

Are you?

Answers

Pages 4-5
Puzzle Holiday!

The Holiday Express bus is here.

Pages 6-7
On the way

The people circled here are going to the Puzzle Holiday Park.

Pages 8-9
Listen carefully

Katy and Tim are in the Puzzlers group. Their activities are seaside fun, circus skills, fun splash pool, animal world and the boating lake. At the end of the day, they will join up with everyone at the funfair. Their route is shown here.

Pages 10-11
Tent trouble

Match the letters to see who is sleeping in each tent.

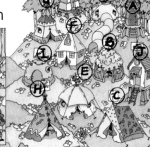

Pages 12-13
Mountain bikes

This path leads to the archery.

This path leads to the seaside.

This path leads to the arts and crafts.

This path leads to the circus tent.

Pages 14-15
Seaside fun

The objects are circled below.

Pages 16-17
Wild woodland walk

The safe way up the paths is shown here.

Pages 18-19
Circus fun

The differences are circled below.

Pages 20-21
Water fun

Greg must take slide 3.

Katy must take slide 1.

Tim must take slide 2.

Sophie must take slide 4.

Pages 22-23
Animal World

The animals' food is circled here.

Pages 24-25
Boating lake

The boats circled here are being called in.

Pages 26-27
Fun at the fair

Yes, all of the groups are here!

Look out for the red holiday hats.

Pages 28-29
Holiday feast

The toffee apples are circled here.

Did you spot everything?
Supreme Spotters' Challenge

Stinky skunks

Did you know?

The friends that Katy and Tim have made in the Puzzle Holiday Park can be found in the other books in this series too!

The chart below shows you how many stinky skunks are hiding on each double page. You can also find out where all the things in the Supreme Spotters' Challenge are hidden.

Pages	Stinky skunks	Supreme Spotters' Challenge
4-5	none	toffee tree
6-7	two	blue pumpkin
8-9	one	spotty rabbit
10-11	four	mouse house
12-13	three	spikey spectacles
14-15	two	lobster
16-17	four	giant lollipop
18-19	one	juggling spider
20-21	two	puzzle parrot
22-23	two	toad on a trike
24-25	three	little yellow dragon!
26-27	two	strange smoke signals
28-29	one	windmill

First published in 1997 by Usborne Publishing Ltd, Usborne House, 83-85 Saffron Hill, London EC1N 8RT, England.

Copyright © 1997 Usborne Publishing Ltd.

The name Usborne and the device ⊕ are Trade Marks of Usborne Publishing Ltd. All rights reserved. No part of this publication may be reproduced, stored in a retrieval system, or transmitted in any form or by any means, electronic, mechanical, photocopying, recording or otherwise, without the prior permission of the publisher.

Printed in Portugal

First published in America August 1997   UE